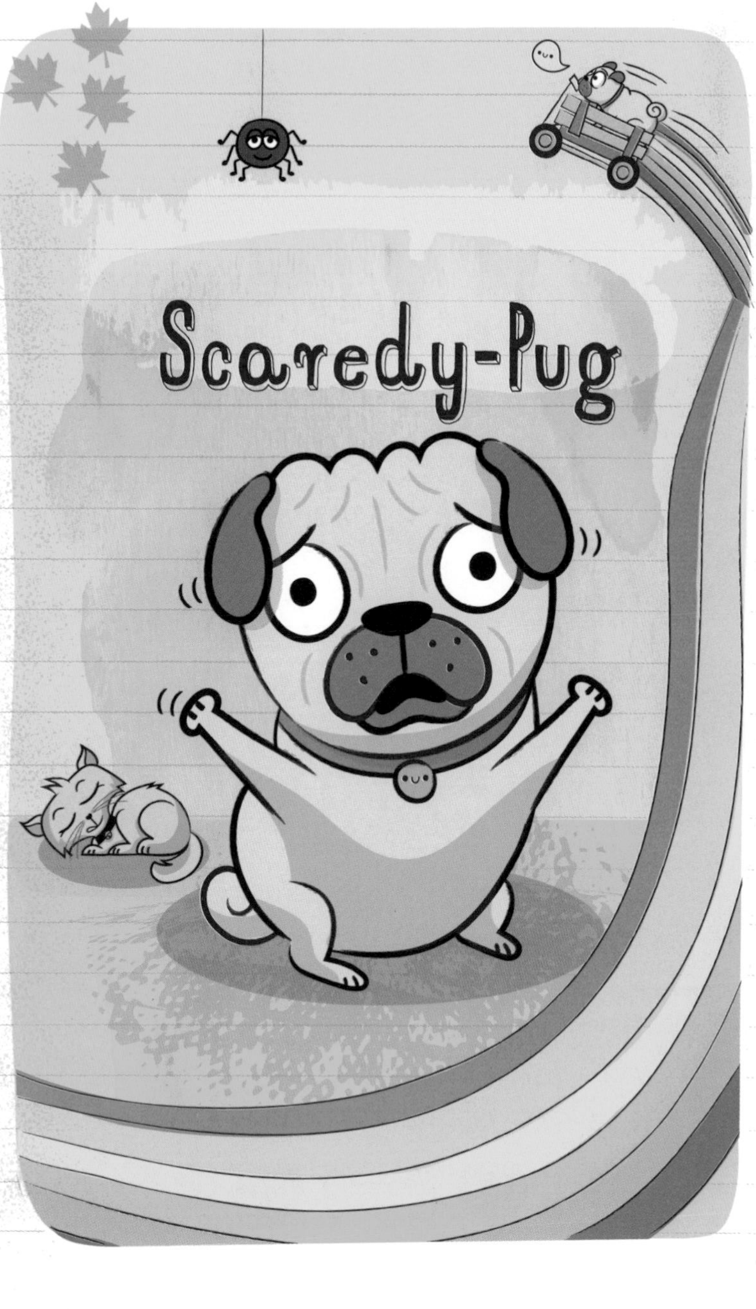
Scaredy-Pug

Read all the Diary of a Pug books!

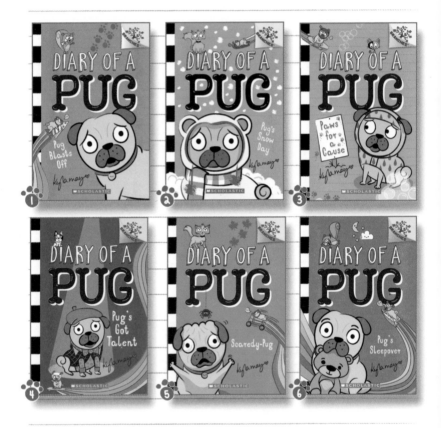

More books coming soon!

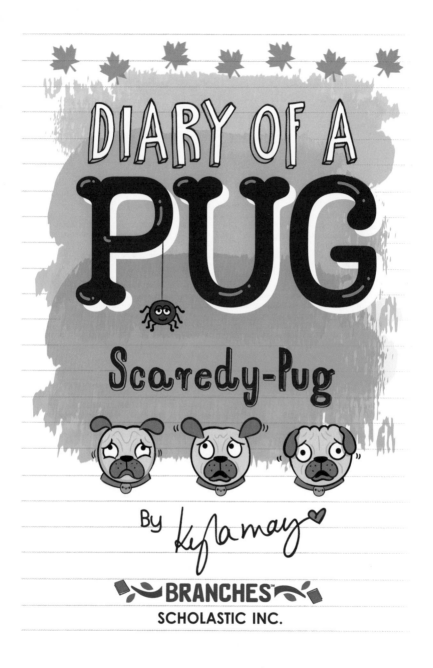

DIARY OF A PUG

Scaredy-Pug

By Kyla May

BRANCHES

SCHOLASTIC INC.

To my new puppy, Harlow.
You bring me so much joy.

Special thanks to Sonia Sander

Art © 2021 by Kyla May
Text © 2021 by Scholastic Inc.

Photos © KylaMay2019

Library of Congress Cataloging-in-Publication Data
Names: May, Kyla, author, illustrator. | May, Kyla. Diary of a pug ; 5. Title: Scaredy pug / by Kyla May.
Description: First edition. | New York : Branches/Scholastic Inc., 2021. | Series: Diary of a pug ; 5 | Summary: Baron von Bubbles (Bub) the pug, Duchess the cat, and their human, Bella, are going to the countryside to visit Bella's grandmother for a few days, where they expect to have fun building forts and dressing up in the attic--but the attic seems to be haunted, and neither Bub nor Duchess can summon up the courage to face the ghost.
Identifiers: LCCN 2020037471 (print) | LCCN 2020037472 (ebook)
ISBN 9781338713442 (paperback) | ISBN 9781338713459 (reinforced library binding)
ISBN 9781338713466 (ebook)
Subjects: LCSH: Pug--Juvenile fiction. | Cats--Juvenile fiction. |
Human-animal relationships--Juvenile fiction. | Haunted houses--Juvenile
fiction. | Fear--Juvenile fiction. | Humorous stories. | CYAC:
Pug--Fiction. | Dogs--Fiction. | Cats--Fiction. | Human-animal
relationships--Fiction. | Haunted houses--Fiction. | Fear--Fiction. |
Humorous stories. | LCGFT: Humorous fiction.
Classification: LCC PZ7.M4535 Sc 2021 (print) | LCC PZ7.M4535 (ebook) |
DDC 813.6 [Fic]--dc23
LC record available at https://lccn.loc.gov/2020037471
LC ebook record available at https://lccn.loc.gov/2020037472

10 9 8 7 6 5 4 3 2   21 22 23 24 25

Printed in China   62
First edition, September 2021
Edited by Katie Woehr
Book design by Kyla May and Christian Zelaya

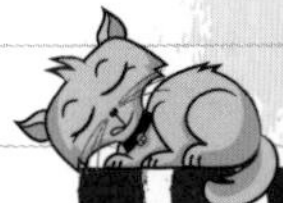

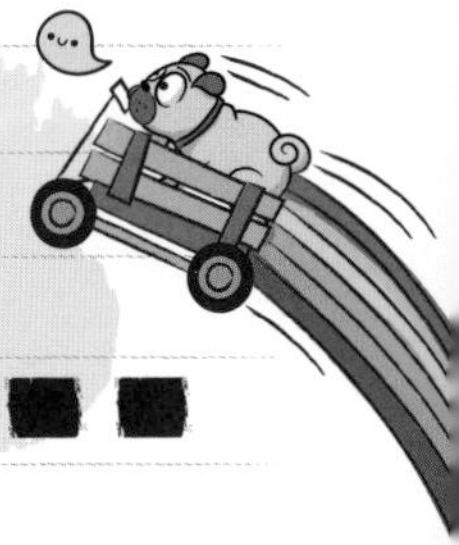

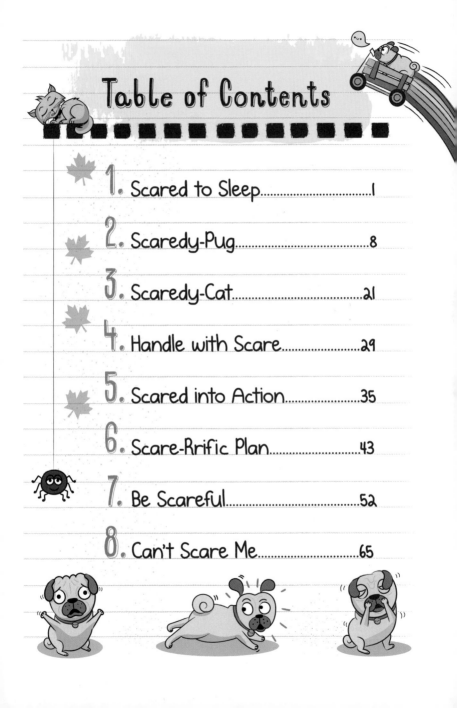

Table of Contents

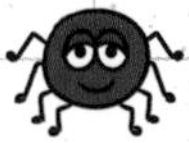

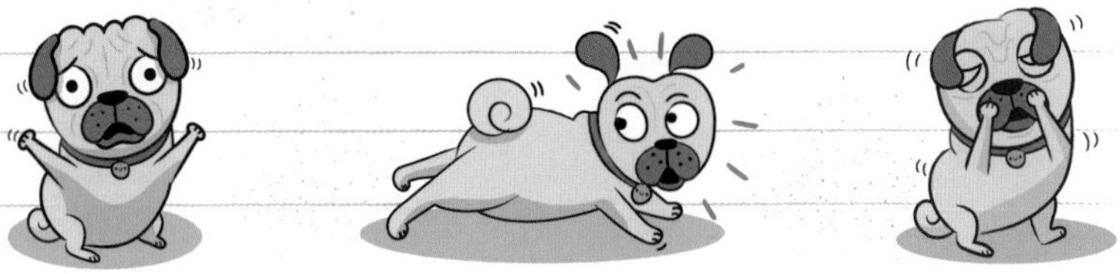

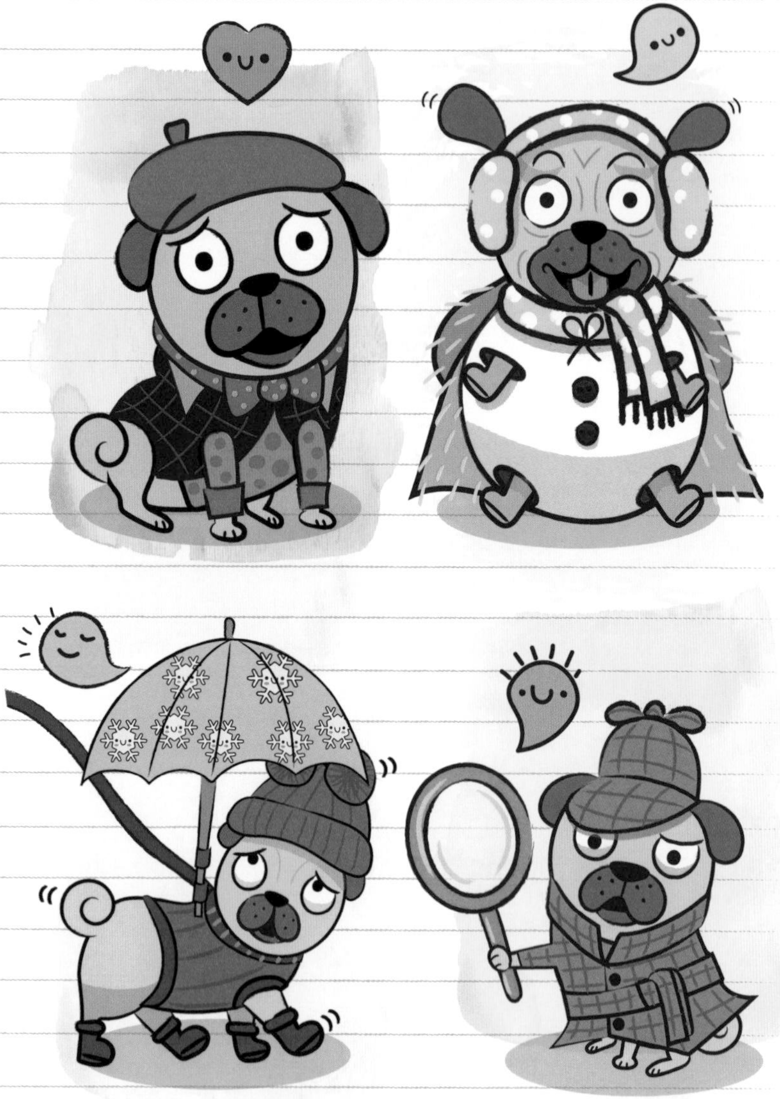

Chapter 1

SCARED TO SLEEP

FRIDAY

Dear Diary,

Knock, knock. Guess who? It's me, your favorite pug, **BUB!**

I've got a bone-chilling mystery to share with you.

But first, here are some things to know about me:

Fashion is my passion.

<u>I make many different faces:</u>

Playtime with Bella Face

Riding in a Car Face

Nervous Face (or I Just Farted Face)

<u>Here are some of my favorite things:</u>

NAP TIME

PEANUT BUTTER TREATS

MY BEST FRIEND,
LUNA

Here are some things that get on my nerves:

And **WATER**, of course! You know I don't like water! Bella laughed so hard the first time I jumped into a bubble bath. I had no idea there was WATER under the bubbles! (That's how I got my full name, by the way—BARON VON BUBBLES.)

Let's get back to my story. When Bella came home from school today, she was super happy.

Bubby, I have a surprise for you!

BELLA'S BAG

SNIFF
SNIFF

Is it peanut butter treats?!

But my nose let me know there weren't any treats in Bella's bag.

Bella was excited because we are taking a trip!

We leave tomorrow!

Where are we going?

I know where. It's fun—I mean, it's awful. You should stay home.

You're coming, too? Great.

Chapter 2

SCAREDY PUG

Dear Diary,

The car was packed. Jack and Luna came to see us off.

> I wish we were going with you.

> Me too. I'd rather take a trip with you than with Duchess.

> Where are you going?

> I still don't know ...

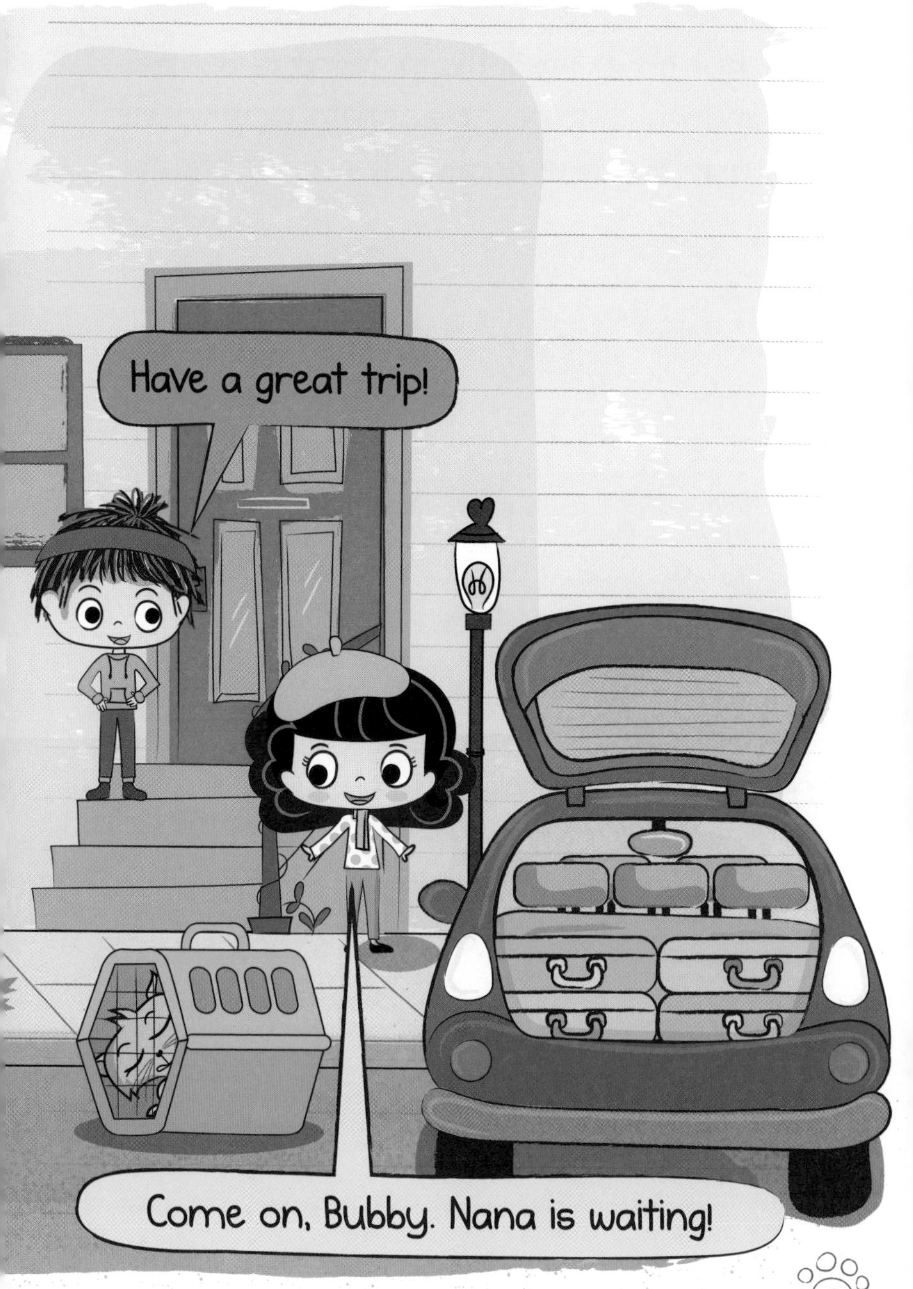
Have a great trip!
Come on, Bubby. Nana is waiting!

I got so excited, Diary. Nana is Bella's grandma. I've never been to her house before. But she makes the best treats.

We're going to Nana's. Woo-hooo!

The more we drove, the more nervous I felt. But guess what?

I forgot about the ghost when we arrived. Nana's house was the best place ever!

There were so many fun things to do! There were . . .

Leaves to jump in!

Bugs to chase!

Sticks to fetch!

I was so excited that I ran into a creek by accident.

Bella took me inside. I THOUGHT she was going to dry me off with a towel like usual. But she kept talking about warming me up with a hot water bottle. Can you believe that? I just got out of the water!

Isn't that better?

Can I take this home?

It turns out hot water bottles are amazing!

Later, Bella took me to her favorite place in Nana's house—the attic.

The attic smelled funny.

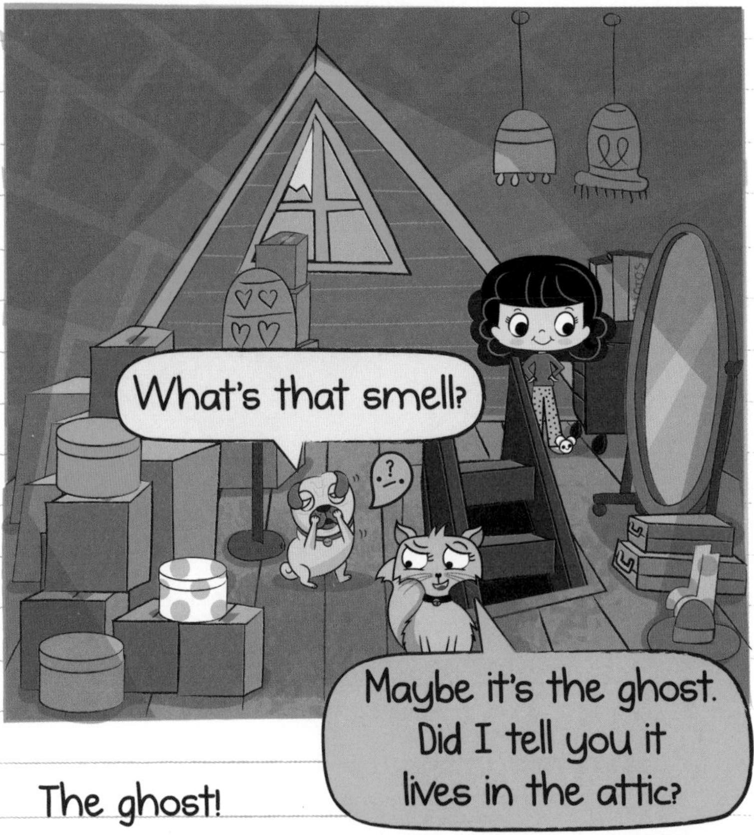
What's that smell?
Maybe it's the ghost. Did I tell you it lives in the attic?

The ghost!

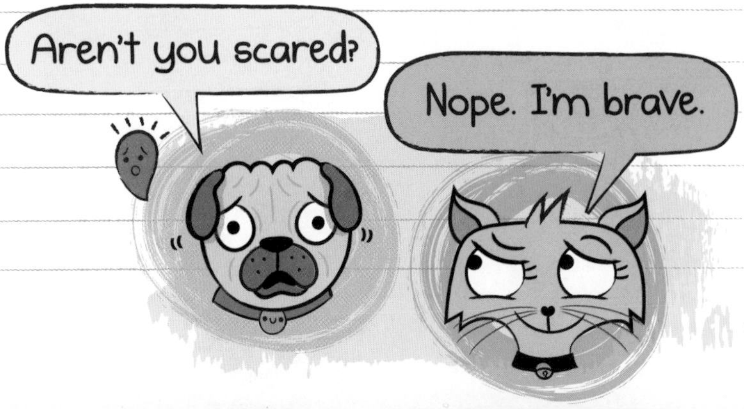
Aren't you scared?
Nope. I'm brave.

But, Diary, Duchess isn't as brave as she says she is. Remember how she freaked out at the pet talent show?

I decided she was making up the ghost story because she wanted the attic all to herself.

Good try, Duchess, but I'm not falling for it.

Suit yourself.

Speaking of suits, Bella said we could play dress-up.

Then we built a fort.

I was having so much fun in the attic that Bella had to drag me downstairs for dinner.

We'll leave the fort up for tomorrow. It's time for dinner now.

Already?

Don't hurry back.

I'm so glad I didn't fall for Duchess's ghost story. I would have missed out on fun with Bella. I can't wait to play in the attic again tomorrow!

Chapter 3

SCAREDY-CAT

SUNDAY

Dear Diary,

Today did not start well. Before the sun rose, a loud BANG from the attic woke us up!

Was that the ghost?!

We went up to check the attic. I told myself the ghost wasn't real, but I was still scared.

I bet it's just Duchess. I hope she's not making a mess.

It's okay, Bubby. That's only a spider.

Our fort was flat as a pancake. Bella thought Duchess knocked down the fort. She started calling for her. I didn't hate seeing Duchess get in trouble.

You naughty kitten, where are you?

Duchess in trouble is worth an early wake-up!

While Bella rebuilt our fort, I went to find Duchess. I wanted to tease her for getting in trouble. But my plan changed when I saw her. Duchess was scared!

What happened?

I heard a loud OOOOOO! Something brushed past me.

Wait. You didn't make up the ghost just to scare me?

No! I mean, yes. But now I think it's REAL!

I didn't know what to believe, Diary. If Duchess had lied earlier, then maybe she was lying now, too.

All of a sudden a *WHOOSH* of air hit us and we saw a shadow on the wall!

Duchess and I raced out of the attic. I ran to Bella's room. Duchess ran to who knows where. I couldn't stop shaking. Bella came to find out what was wrong.

What's the matter? Did something scare you?

A GHOST!!

Come out for a cuddle, Mr. Scaredy-Pug.

Bella took super-good care of me for the rest of the day. She even asked Nana to make my favorite treats.

Silly Bubby. Have another treat.

Yum! Cuddles AND treats!

It was a perfect afternoon.

But then I realized something . . . Bella didn't know about the ghost! She might want to play in the attic tomorrow. I'll have to stop her to keep her safe!

Chapter 4

HANDLE WITH SCARE

MONDAY

Dear Diary,

I hardly slept a wink last night trying to figure out how to keep Bella away from the attic. Thank goodness today was sunny. Bella couldn't wait to get outside.

Come on, sleepyhead. Let's go play.

Morning already?! I'm going to need a nap later.

We stopped for breakfast before going outside. Duchess wasn't there. I hated to admit it, but I was worried about her. She was pretty freaked out yesterday.

Sweet Duchess must be sleeping in.

SWEET Duchess?!?! I don't think so.

But I hope she's okay . . .

DOG FOOD

CAT FOOD

WATER

Bella and I had a picnic. Then we took a nap in the sun.

This would be even better if Duchess were here. Let's go find her.

Do we have to?

Back inside, we looked for Duchess. We found her hiding under a chair. She jumped when we arrived.

She calmed down after she saw it was us.

Something really scared you two yesterday.

Well, I'm over it. This scaredy-cat isn't.

What do you know?!

It's okay, Duchess. You can come out when you're ready.

Bella and I went back outside. We had a wagon race. (I won, of course.) Then Bella shared some news.

Looks like it's going to rain tomorrow.

RAIN?! NOOOOO!!!

It was easy to keep Bella out of the attic today, Diary. How will I do it when we can't go outside?

Chapter 5

SCARED INTO ACTION

TUESDAY

Dear Diary,

This morning, I decided I needed Duchess's help if I was going to keep Bella out of the attic. I found her under the chair.

It's raining outside. Will you help me keep Bella out of the attic?

Help you?! No way! You'll have to choose: rain or ghost.

I hate the rain, but I hate ghosts WAY more. Bella was on her way to the attic when I found her. So I used my no-fail move.

We suited up and headed out. We splashed through puddles, made mud cakes, and caught raindrops. I hated every minute.

We should play in the rain more often!

Don't count on it.

We played until we were too cold and wet to move.

Let's go inside, Bub. Nana gave me some old pearls for dress-up. We can play in the attic.

Inside sounded nice, Diary. But I freaked out when Bella mentioned the attic.

Why are you so afraid of the attic, Bub? There's nothing to be scared of up there.

All of a sudden, thunder sounded in the sky. BOOM! Then something flew past the inside of the attic window!

We raced into the house and joined Duchess under the chair.

Look who the scaredy-cats are now.

Zip it, furball.

So much for playing in the attic . . .

I was glad Bella finally knew about the ghost. Now she wouldn't want to play in the attic.

Let's curl up with Nana in front of the fireplace.

You don't have to ask me twice!

But there's something we have to do first.

Oh, Diary. I didn't know the day could get any worse.

Chapter 6

SCARE-RRIFIC PLAN

WEDNESDAY

Dear Diary,

After three sleepless nights, I slept in. Bella was eating breakfast when I woke up.

Hello, sleepyhead. What should we do today?

DOG FOOD

WATER

Anything without rain or a ghost.

I was finishing my breakfast when Duchess snuck up on me.

Eeeekkk!

Welcome to life beyond the chair, Duchess. Wait. Where's your collar?

You lost the annoying bell collar? Oh darn.

Hey! I've had that collar since Bella brought me home.

Bella was really upset about the collar.
We searched the whole house.

Well, almost the whole house.

What if it's in the . . .

Don't say the attic.

I'm not going up there.

But Bella wouldn't give up. The collar meant too much to her.

Ghost or no ghost, we have to check the attic. Will you come with me?

Okay. But I'm doing this for you. Not for Duchess.

Gee, thanks.

Okay! Today, we prepare. Tomorrow, we face the ghost.

Bella named our mission OPERATION BELL COLLAR. There were many things to do to get ready.

STEP ONE: Gather your armor.

STEP TWO: Make a plan to search for the collar.

ATTIC ↓

WINDOW

BOXES

BOXES

PHOTO ALBUMS

BELLA'S JOB: Look for the collar.

STAIRS

FORT

BUB'S JOB: Do skateboard tricks to distract the ghost.

DUCHESS'S JOB: Watch for the ghost and meow if you see it.

OLD MATTRESS

CLOTHES RACK (DRESS-UPS)

WINDOW

STEP THREE: Make a plan for facing the ghost.

If the ghost shows up, I'll throw this blanket over it.

Duchess, you toss that ball of yarn at the ghost. That should tangle it up.

Bub, you bark to scare it away.

STEP FOUR: Practice the plan.

Pretend the chair is the ghost. Ready, go!

RUFF! RUFF!

R-r-r-o-o-w-w!

STEP FIVE: Celebrate!

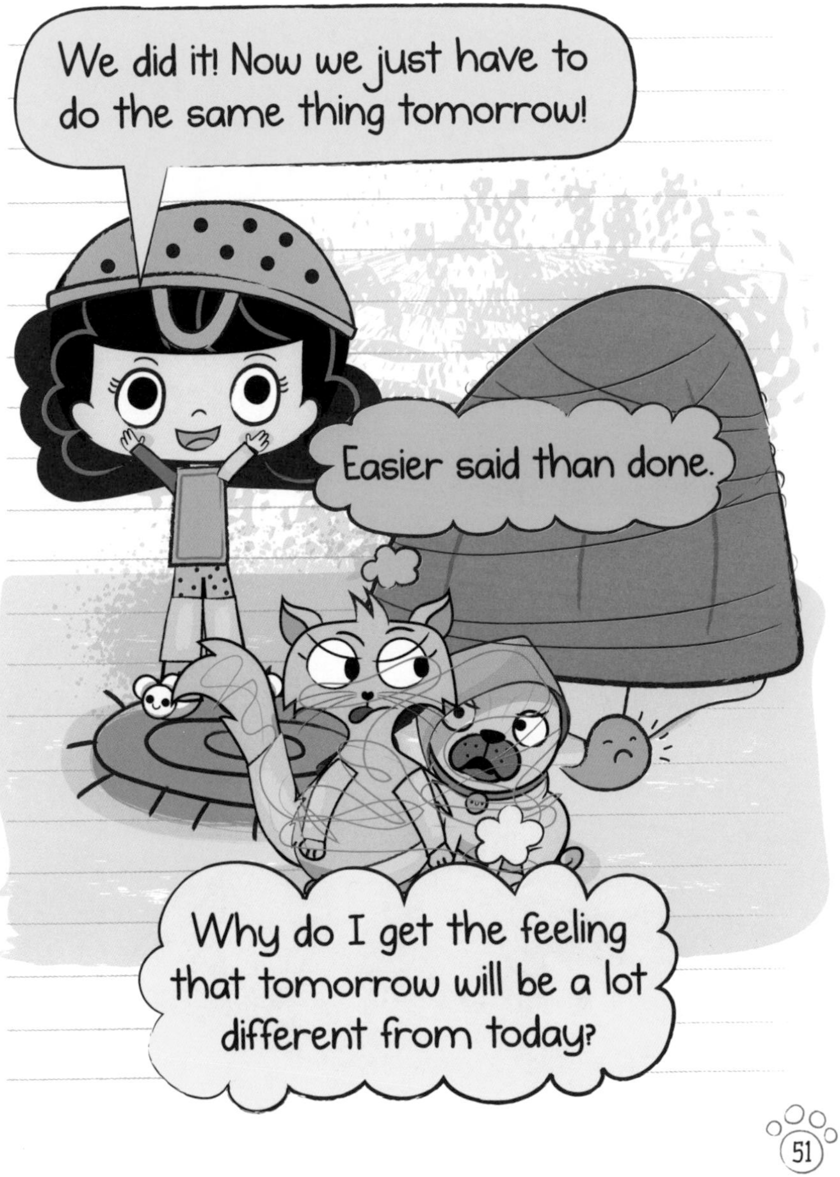
We did it! Now we just have to do the same thing tomorrow!
Easier said than done.
Why do I get the feeling that tomorrow will be a lot different from today?

Chapter 7

BE SCAREFUL

THURSDAY

Dear Diary,

Today was the day for Operation Bell Collar. Bella was ready to go. Duchess and I were feeling nervous.

Let's do this!

Do we have to?

Can I change my mind?

We climbed the attic stairs.

But guess what? There was no sign of the ghost. The first part of our plan—to search for the collar—went fine.

Except Bella didn't find the collar.

I'm sorry, Duchess. I don't see it anywhere.

Maybe the ghost stole the collar?

Well . . . thanks for trying.

Just then a WHOOSH of air rushed past us. Duchess screamed . . . and bolted down the stairs.

I wanted to be brave, Diary. I tried to bark, but nothing came out. I was too scared. I grabbed Bella's blanket and ran to hide.

Bub! I need that for the ghost!

I failed, Diary. I left Bella to face the ghost alone. She was so brave. I really was a scaredy-pug.

There was another WHOOSH of wind and a flapping noise. Then TWO shadows flew across the wall!

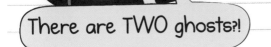

There are TWO ghosts?!

Bella jumped under the blanket with me. She was ready to quit.

We didn't plan on TWO ghosts! Let's get out of here!

Fine with me!

But as Bella climbed out, she knocked into a stack of boxes and I heard something. Duchess's bell! The collar was stuck under a box! The ghosts started OOOOOOing. I wanted to run, too. But I couldn't leave now. I tugged and tugged on the collar.

TING-A-LING

The collar finally came free. Boxes
tumbled down.

I wiggled out from under the boxes. I was ready to run for the door, but Bella was frozen.

It was a mama owl and a baby owl, Diary! The cutest little creatures you've ever seen!

I think we found the ghosts, Bub. They must have come through the broken window.

They've built a nest in the attic.

Hooray! We found the ghosts and Duchess's collar, too. Operation Bell Collar worked!

Chapter 8

CAN'T SCARE ME

FRIDAY

Dear Diary,

It was our last day at Nana's house. I piled my toys by Bella's bag.

Bear—check! Skateboard—check! Oh! I need fresh treats.

Last night, Bella told Nana about our attic adventure. Nana made me treats for the ride home this morning!

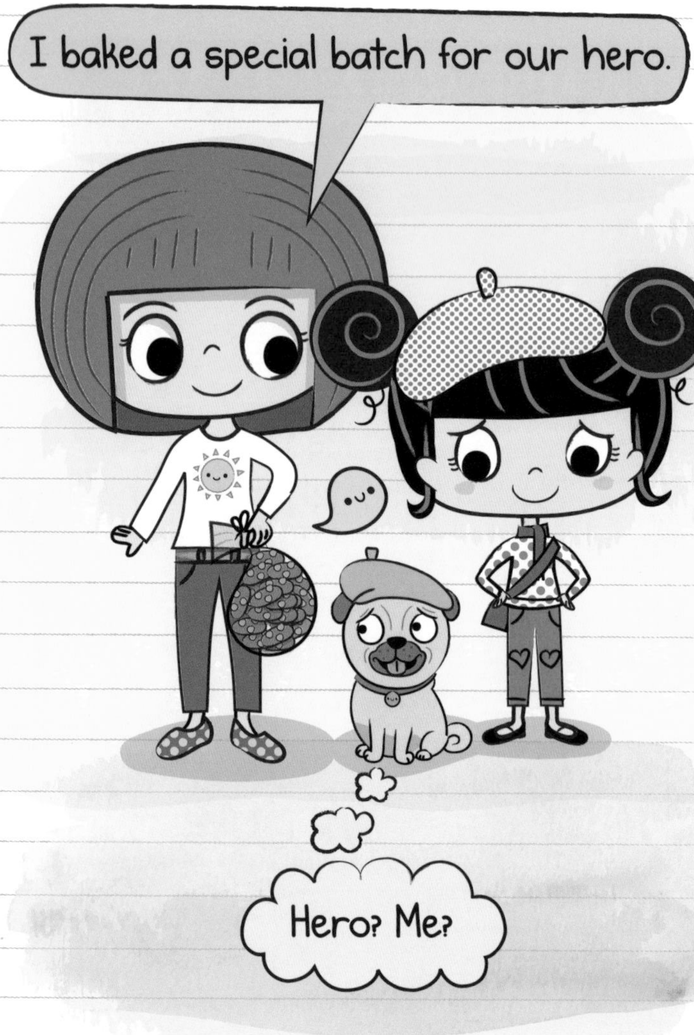
I baked a special batch for our hero.
Hero? Me?

I heard Duchess's bell as she strolled into the kitchen. I hate to admit it—I had missed that sound.

We went up to the attic. Nana wanted to meet the owls and we had gifts for them.

This is Nana's old necklace. It will make your nest sparkle!

Here are a few of my treats.

Once the baby owl is ready to leave the nest, I'll get that window fixed.

Owl poop sure is stinky!

Our time was up. We hopped in the car and headed home. I told Duchess how she could repay me—by feeding me treats all the way home!

Jack and Luna were waiting for us when we got home. We told them all about our trip.

You won't believe this, Diary. As soon as we got out of the car, Nutz ran toward what was left of my treats!

The nerve of that squirrel, Diary! But an annoying squirrel is nothing once you've faced a ghost! I chased after Nutz to get my treats back. I'm a SUPER-PUG, after all!

About the Creator

Kyla May is an Australian illustrator, writer, and designer. In addition to books, Kyla creates animation. She lives by the beach in Victoria, Australia, with her three daughters and two dogs. The character of Bub was inspired by her daughter's pug called Bear.

HOW MUCH DO YOU KNOW ABOUT

DIARY OF A PUG

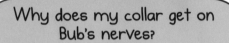

Scaredy-Pug?

Why does my collar get on Bub's nerves?

Why does Bub love Nana?

There are three things that make Bub and Duchess believe there is a ghost: Something they HEAR, something they FEEL, and something they SEE. What are those three things?

Something unexpected happens on pages 59–60. What makes Bella dive under the blanket?

The owls' shadows looked like ghosts. Can you move your body to make your shadow look like a ghost? What other things can you make your shadow look like?